The Sleepover Club

Have you been invited to all these sleepovers?

Sleepover Girls

go Designer

by Narinder Dhami

Collins

An imprint of HarperCollinsPublishers

The Sleepover Club ® is a Registered Trademark of
HarperCollins*Publishers* Ltd

First published in Great Britain by Collins in 1999
Collins is an imprint of HarperCollins*Publishers* Ltd
77-85 Fulham Palace Road, Hammersmith,
London, W6 8JB

The HarperCollins website address is
www.fireandwater.com

5 7 9 8 6 4

Text copyright © Narinder Dhami 1999

Original series characters, plotlines
and settings © Rose Impey 1997

ISBN 0 00 675422 8

The author asserts the moral right to
be identified as the author of the work.

Printed and bound in Great Britain by
Omnia Books Limited, Glasgow

Sleepover Kit List

1. Sleeping bag
2. Pillow
3. Pyjamas or a nightdress
4. Slippers
5. Toothbrush, toothpaste, soap etc
6. Towel
7. Teddy
8. A creepy story
9. Food for a midnight feast:
   chocolate, crisps, sweets, biscuits.
   In fact anything you like to eat.
10. Torch
11. Hairbrush
12. Hair things like a bobble or hairband,
    if you need them
13. Clean knickers and socks
14. Change of clothes for the next day
15. Sleepover diary and membership card

CHAPTER ONE

Hi. It's me. What do you mean, *who*? Rosie, of course! OK, so I sound a bit miserable, and I'll tell you why. At the moment I've got two *big* problems: 1) I'm sitting on a lump of ice and it's freezing my bottom off, and 2)—

"Come on, Rosie-Posie, get up!" Kenny yelled, skating towards me at about a hundred miles an hour. I gasped, and scrambled to my feet quickly to get out of the way, but Kenny just dug her blades into the ice and came to a stop about two centimetres from my nose. What a show-off. I began to wobble from one side to the other, then my legs slowly started moving apart, and I couldn't stop them. I did the splits like Bambi does in the film, and sat down on the ice again.

"Nice one, Rosie!" Frankie said, skating smoothly up to me. "You didn't tell us you could do tricks!"

"Oh, ha ha," I muttered, rubbing my sore behind, "I'd laugh if that was the slightest bit funny."

"Oh, come on, Rosie, don't be such a sad case!" Kenny grabbed hold of one of my arms, Frankie took the other and between them they pulled me to my feet. "What's biting you? You've been in a right mood all afternoon!"

Before I could say anything, Fliss and Lyndz skated over. You remember everyone in the Sleepover Club, don't you? You should do, by now! There's me, Kenny, Frankie, Fliss and Lyndz. We take it in turns to have sleepovers every week at each other's houses, and it was *my* turn tonight. That was my second problem…

I guess you remember what happened. When we moved to Cuddington, my dad bought this massive house, and we were all going to live in it like a happy-ever-after family – that's my mum and dad, me, my sister Tiffany, my brother Adam and our dog Jenny. The house needed *loads* doing to it, but my dad's a builder, so that was all right. Anyway, he started pulling off all the old wallpaper and taking up the carpets and knocking down walls, then he suddenly decided he'd had enough, and he went off to live with his girlfriend. Since then he keeps promising that he's going to fix the house for us, but he's hardly done anything. I love my dad to bits, but he drives me *mad*.

"Look out!" Kenny screeched as Fliss and Lyndz headed straight towards us. Fliss wasn't very good at stopping, and because she and Lyndz were holding hands, she was dragging Lyndz along with her. Alarmed, Kenny and Frankie let go of my arms again, and I collapsed in a heap. Unfortunately, I grabbed at the hood of Kenny's Leicester City FC sweatshirt as I fell, and pulled her down on to the ice next to me. Fliss and Lyndz managed to avoid us, but not Frankie, and the three of them landed in an untidy pile right on top of me and Kenny.

"Oi! Get off!" Kenny roared, "you're suffocating us!"

Frankie, Lyndz and Fliss could hardly move, they were laughing so much. It was all right for them. They weren't at the bottom of the heap like I was.

"Are you girls all right?" called Frankie's mum from the side of the rink.

Frankie gave her a thumbs-up as we all climbed to our feet.

"I'm going to be black and blue after this," I grumbled. Ice-skating just wasn't my thing. But then, nothing ever goes right for me...

"Oh, come on, Rosie, it's a good laugh!" Frankie said with a grin.

"You'll soon get better after you've been a few more times," Lyndz said kindly.

Fliss stared at me suspiciously. "What's the matter, Rosie? You've got a right face on you."

"That's what I said," Kenny chimed in. "So what's the story?"

I felt a bit embarrassed and shuffled my feet, but *that* was a mistake because I nearly fell over again.

"It's my dad," I mumbled. "He promised he was going to decorate my bedroom this week, and he didn't."

"Well, great big fat hairy deal!" Kenny shrugged. "So what's new? You've been waiting for him to do it for months!"

Frankie and Lyndz both elbowed Kenny in the ribs so hard that she nearly fell over, and I glared at her.

"I know," I snapped. I guess I don't like anyone else criticising my dad, even though he gets on my nerves. But it's true. My bedroom's a tip, and it's been like that for *ever*. When I first met the others, I didn't even want them to come round to our house and see just what a mess it is. "But he *promised* me he'd do it before the sleepover tonight. We even went out and bought all the wallpaper and paint last week-end."

"You didn't say anything about that," Lyndz remarked.

I had a horrible big fat lump in my throat. "I wanted it to be a surprise when you slept over," I muttered.

"So why hasn't he done it?" Fliss asked sympathetically.

"He's gone on holiday with his girlfriend," I said, and the others groaned.

"What, *again*?" Kenny said, raising her eyebrows. "Your dad's the Holiday King!"

"I know." I couldn't argue with that. "He's gone to Majorca for a week with her. He *says* he'll do my bedroom when he gets back…"

The others just looked at me. They didn't say anything, but I knew what they were thinking. I was thinking exactly the same thing myself. *Some hope.*

"Girls, what are you doing standing around?" Mrs Thomas was waving to us from the seats at the side of the rink. "If you've had enough, we might as well go."

"Another ten minutes, Mum," Frankie called back. Then she turned to the rest of us. "Come on, let's go round another couple of times."

"I think I'll give it a miss," I said gloomily. I knew I was being a pain in the bottom – I'd fallen over so many times, I *had* a pain in the bottom – but I was really fed up about my bedroom. I'd been dying to get it finished before the sleepover tonight. But it was still all bare walls, no carpet and hardly any furniture. I was sick of it.

"Oh, no you don't!" Kenny grabbed my arm. "Come on, let's play trains!"

"What?" I said. "Aren't we a bit too old for that?"

"*Funny*. Listen, we all line up and hold on to each other's waists," Kenny explained. "I'll go at the front, and pull you along."

"OK, but don't go too fast," Fliss said nervously.

"Lyndz, you stand behind Rosie so that she's got something soft to fall on!" Frankie said with a grin.

"Thanks a lot!" Lyndz retorted.

So we all lined up behind Kenny – me, then Lyndz, then Fliss and Frankie at the end. Then we all set off round the rink, hanging on to

13

each other. At least this way I didn't have to do any skating, because Kenny was towing us all along.

"Hey, did anyone see *Designer Rooms* last night?" Kenny called over her shoulder as we skimmed round the edge of the rink. "It was brilliant! One of the rooms looked worse than it did before they re-decorated it!"

"Kenny!" Fliss hissed from behind me.

Kenny ignored her. "Then, when they brought the woman who owns the house to see it when it was finished, she burst into tears! She said she'd never seen anything so horrible in all her life!"

"Honestly, Kenny," Fliss snapped. "If your brain was as big as your mouth, you might have a bit more common sense!"

Kenny turned round, an injured look on her face. "What?"

"I don't think Rosie wants to talk about *Designer Rooms*, Kenny," Frankie called from the end of the line. "You know, it's all about *decorating*?"

"Oh yeah, sorry, Rosie," Kenny said over

her shoulder. "But it was a real laugh!"

That was when I had my really cool idea.

"Hey, I've just had a really cool idea!" I gasped. "Why don't I write to the *Designer Rooms* programme and ask them if they could come and decorate my bedroom?"

"No chance," Kenny called back. "They said last night that they were getting *thousands* of letters from people who wanted to be on the programme, and not to send any more."

"Oh, rats!" That was just about my last hope of getting my bedroom decorated gone down the drain…

"Can't your mum do it for you?" Lyndz asked.

"She's pretty busy with her college work," I muttered. "She hasn't got time."

"Well, what about your grandparents or someone like that?" Frankie persisted.

"There isn't anyone," I snapped. I knew the others were only trying to help, but they were really making me feel worse. I was stuck with my disgusting bedroom, and that was that.

Kenny suddenly came to a dead stop right

in front of us. "Hey! Extra-special, double-brilliant, triple-coo-ell Kenny brainwave!" she yelled. "Why don't *we* decorate Rosie's bedroom tonight at the sleepover?"

No-one had a chance to say anything just then. We all crashed slap-bang into Kenny, one after the other, and keeled over like a row of dominoes.

CHAPTER TWO

"I think it's a *wicked* idea, Kenny!" I said eagerly, as we sat at the side of the rink, taking our skates off. "Do you really think we can do it?"

"'Course we can!" Kenny said, shrugging her shoulders. "We've all watched *Designer Rooms* loads of times, haven't we? How hard can it be to slap a bit of paint around?"

Then Kenny and I noticed that Frankie, Fliss and Lyndz were looking a bit sick.

"What's up with you bunch of wimps?" Kenny asked crossly. "Poor old Rosie needs our help. Now are you up for this or not?"

"Kenny, I don't know much about decorating," Frankie said with a frown. "But I know it isn't as easy as it looks."

"I thought you were helping your mum and dad get the spare room ready for the baby," Kenny pointed out. (You haven't forgotten that Frankie's mum's pregnant, have you? Frankie's wanted a brother or sister for *ages*, so it's mega-cool.)

"Yeah, I am," Frankie retorted. "That's how I know decorating's not easy. My dad did the wallpapering yesterday, and he didn't make the paste thick enough. When we went in there this morning, half the paper had fallen off the walls!"

"Frankie's right," Lyndz chimed in. "You know my dad does a lot of DIY, and he's pretty good at it. But things are always going wrong – once he knocked himself out with a hammer!"

Kenny gave a snort of disgust. "You lot have got no sense of adventure! What about you, Flissy?"

Fliss wrinkled her nose. "Decorating's really

messy, isn't it?" she said. "I don't want to get paint all over me."

My heart sank. Kenny and I couldn't do the decorating on our own. If the others wouldn't join in, that was the end of that.

"Oh, never mind," I muttered in a bit of a trembly voice. "I suppose I'll just have to wait till my dad gets back from Majorca…"

"No way José!" Kenny patted me sympathetically on the shoulder, and then glared round at the others. "Look, don't be weeds all of your life, you lot! Are you going to help me and Rosie out or not?"

We all looked at each other.

"Oh, all right," Frankie said at last, and Lyndz and Fliss nodded too.

"Thanks, guys!" I said, relieved.

"Don't thank us till you've seen the finished result!" Frankie warned me, but Kenny thumped her on the back.

"Don't get your knickers in a knot, Frankie!" she said. "Rosie's bedroom's going to look a million times better than anything on *Designer Rooms*!"

19

I grinned round at the others. My bedroom was going to be decorated at last! I could hardly believe it.

"How are we going to do it without someone hearing us?" Lyndz asked doubtfully. "We're bound to make a noise."

"Oh, get off!" Kenny scoffed, rolling her eyes. "We're only sticking up wallpaper and doing a bit of painting! We'll be dead quiet."

"Anyway, Adam and Tiffany are both away this week-end," I added. My brother Adam, who's in a wheelchair because he's got cerebral palsy, goes to a special school, and he'd gone on an adventure week-end with some of the other pupils. My big sister Tiff had arranged to stay overnight with her best mate, who was having a party. "So it's just me and Mum. And you know she doesn't bother much if we make a bit of a row."

"What are we going to wear?" Fliss asked anxiously. "I'm not painting in my brand-new pyjamas!"

"I'll lend you some old clothes," I said quickly. We were going straight to my house from the ice rink, and the others had brought their sleepover kits with them.

"Come on, girls." Mrs Thomas came over to hurry us up. "I promised Rosie's mum I'd have you there by five." She glanced round at us. "You lot look like you're plotting something. What's going on?"

"Nothing, Mrs Thomas," we all said innocently. That's the trouble with Frankie's mum. She's just a bit too sharp.

"I hope not," Mrs Thomas said briskly, "because when you start putting your heads together like that, it usually means trouble!"

I couldn't help starting to worry then. Just a bit. I mean, I'd never done any kind of decorating before. The only thing I'd ever painted were pictures at school (and I wasn't too hot at that either). Still, I told myself, Frankie and Lyndz knew what to do because they'd helped their parents lots of times. And as Kenny said, how hard could slapping a bit of paint around *be*?

* * *

"You want to go to bed *now*?" My mum stared at us in amazement. "But it's only half-past eight!"

"But we're dead tired, Mrs Cartwright!" Kenny said pathetically, and we all started yawning and rubbing our eyes.

"All right, all right, spare me the amateur dramatics!" my mum said, shaking her head. "Off you go – and whatever you're up to, don't make too much noise about it. I've got an essay to write."

"Excellent!" I said in a low voice to Kenny. "That means she'll be working in the study – and that's right over the other side of the house."

We all piled into the living-room so that the others could grab their sleepover bags. Since we'd got back from the ice rink, we'd done all the usual sleepover-type things. We'd had tea, and, because it was Saturday, we'd watched *Gladiators*, and then we'd played our own Gladiator games. Kenny had come up with a new one. Two people stood on one leg on chairs facing each other, and then they whacked each other with cushions until one fell off. It was really radical.

Although we were having a laugh, as usual, I could hardly wait to get upstairs and get started on my bedroom. I reckoned I'd put up with it looking gross for too long already.

"Come on then!" Kenny yelled, slinging her sleepover bag over her shoulder. We all charged up the stairs and burst into my bedroom, giggling and pushing each other out of the way. As soon as we were inside, everyone stopped and stared. The walls were plaster, the woodwork was scraped bare, and there was a pile of stuff lying in the corner.

"What's all *that*?" Kenny asked.

"That's my dad's decorating gear," I explained. "He left it here."

"So we've got everything we need – excellent!" Kenny went over to have a look, and picked up a roll of wallpaper. "Hey, Frankie, check this out – this is cool!"

The wallpaper I'd chosen was a lilac colour with little silver flowers on it, and I'd matched it with a darker purple paint for the woodwork. (Dad had been talking about a silvery-grey carpet too, but he hadn't got it yet. *Typical*.) I couldn't wait to see what everything looked like together.

"Come on, then, let's get started!" Kenny said, grabbing a packet of wallpaper paste.

"Hold on a sec, Kenny!" said Frankie. "We need to decide who's going to do what."

"And we've got to decide what we're going to do first," Lyndz added.

"*And* we need to change our clothes," Fliss said firmly.

"Oh, you lot are so bor-ing!" Kenny moaned, putting the wallpaper down. "Give us some old clothes then, Rosie."

I went over to my big wardrobe, and pulled out an old pair of leggings and a sweatshirt for myself. I didn't have anything much for the others though – until I remembered my old bag of dressing-up clothes which was pushed right to the back. I dragged it out and put it in the middle of the room.

"Oh, wow!" said Frankie, putting her hand into the bag and pulling out a big hat with flowers all over it. "This is brilliant!"

Fliss peered into the bag, and let out an ear-shattering scream. "There's— there's a *head* in there!"

"Calm down, Fliss!" Lyndz said quickly. "It's just a wig!" She grabbed hold of the long dark hair and pulled it out. "Rosie, what *is* all this stuff?"

"It's my dressing-up clothes," I explained. "I used to play with them when I was little."

Kenny groaned. "We're going to look like right wallies doing the decorating in dressing-up clothes!" Then her eyes lit up as she pounced on a pair of outsized bright blue dungarees that used to belong to my mum. "Cool! I'll have these!"

A few minutes later everyone was ready. Fliss had found a gold and black evening dress which was about ten sizes too big for her, and she was wearing the long black wig as well. Kenny had put the dungarees on, although they were miles too long for her and she kept tripping over the ends. Lyndz was wrapped in my dad's old dressing-gown, and Frankie was wearing our Tiff's old school blazer and the flowery hat. I was feeling a bit left out in my boring sweatshirt and leggings, so I looked in the bag, found a pink woolly hat and put that on.

"I reckon we're the coolest gang of decorators ever!" Kenny said, as she walked over to pick up a roll of wallpaper and tripped over her dungaree bottoms for the fourth time.

"We'd better get started," Lyndz said. "We've wasted loads of time already."

"D'you think we'll finish it all tonight?" I asked doubtfully. My bedroom's really big, and I was beginning to wonder if we'd bitten off more than we could chew.

"Yeah, 'course!" said Kenny, at exactly the same moment as Frankie and Lyndz said, "No chance!"

"We'll finish it!" Kenny insisted, ripping the cellophane off the wallpaper. "Hey, look at this, guys!" She held up the wallpaper, and let it unroll down to the floor really fast. Unfortunately, Fliss's foot was in the way.

"Ow! Ow! My toe!" Fliss squealed, hopping round the room, doubled up in agony. "I'm going to kill you, Kenny!"

"Well, I don't care if we don't finish it," I said, glancing round at the mess. "It can't look any worse than it does now!"

You know what? I was dead wrong.

CHAPTER THREE

"So what do we do first then?" I asked. No-one answered. Instead, everyone stared at Lyndz, who turned pink.

"What are you all looking at?"

"You! You're the expert!" Kenny told her.

"Oh. Well…" Lyndz frowned and looked round the room. "First we've got to paint the woodwork, and let that dry before we start the wallpapering."

Kenny pulled a face. "Oh, knickers to that! I want to wallpaper – I'm not into boring old paint!"

"Why don't Lyndz and Frankie paint one

side of the room, and me, you and Fliss can start papering on the other?" I suggested.

"Good one!" Kenny said immediately. "That OK with you, Flissy?"

"What?" Fliss hadn't heard a word because she was too busy admiring her dress and wig in my mirror.

"I said, do you want to help me and Rosie with the wallpapering?" Kenny repeated loudly, rolling her eyes at me.

"Yeah, OK," Fliss nodded, parading up and down like a supermodel. "I think I look good with black hair, what do you reckon?"

Kenny groaned, and picked up a bucket and a packet of wallpaper paste. "This isn't a fashion show, Fliss! Come and help me mix up the paste."

While Kenny and Fliss went to the bathroom to get some water, Lyndz and Frankie found some brushes, and began to lever the lid off the tin of purple paint. Meanwhile, I set up the pasting table. I was beginning to get pretty excited – things were really starting to happen!

You could say that again. When Kenny and Fliss came back from the bathroom carrying the bucket, Kenny had bits of paste in her hair, and Fliss's wig was looking pretty sticky too.

"I *told* you not to stir it so hard!" Fliss was saying crossly.

"Well, I had to mix it up properly, didn't I?" Kenny retorted, putting the bucket of paste down on the floor. "Hey, look! Frankie and Lyndz have already started painting!"

Lyndz and Frankie were getting on with it, slapping the paint on to the skirting-boards and doing pretty well. The colour looked even better out of the tin than in it.

"Right, Rosie, you can cut and paste," Kenny said, shoving the roll of wallpaper into my hand. "Fliss can help me hang it."

"You've got paste in my wig, Kenny, you dork!" Fliss grumbled, walking backwards so that she could see herself in the mirror. Big mistake. She didn't notice the bucket of paste on the floor behind her.

"Aargh!" Fliss stepped right into the bucket,

and her left foot disappeared into the thick paste with a loud squelching noise. It was like something out of a comedy film, I can tell you. "Help!" she squealed frantically. "Get me out of here!"

Kenny and I rushed over to her, but we weren't much use because we were killing ourselves laughing, and so were Lyndz and Frankie. Fliss managed to pull herself free, and glared at us, her face red.

"Which stupid idiot put that bucket there?"

"You did," Kenny said quickly. "Come on, Rosie, cut a piece of wallpaper and we can get started."

I unrolled the wallpaper and cut off a really long piece, to make sure it would fit. Then I pasted it all over.

"OK – here goes!" Kenny said confidently. She picked up the sticky wallpaper at one end and tried to lift it off the table. But it was so long, she couldn't hold it up. It dropped right over her, and covered her from head to foot.

"Help!" Kenny yelled, trying to pull it off but

getting more and more tangled up, "I can't see!"

Fliss and I hurried over to her, but we couldn't do much because Kenny was dancing round madly, trying to get the wallpaper off herself. She managed it at last – by ripping it in half.

"Oh, great!" I said, looking at the torn bits of paper. "We can't use that now!"

"Never mind, there's plenty more," Kenny gasped, pink in the face. "Cut another piece, will you, Rosie?"

"You should've stuck to painting, Kenny!" Frankie said smugly, and she and Lyndz started to giggle. They were getting on really fast – and I was glad to see that at least *something* was going right.

I cut another piece of paper, and this time I made sure it was a lot shorter than the last one. I pasted it and gave it to Kenny, who climbed up the ladder and stuck it against the wall. Guess what? It wasn't long enough.

"You've cut it too short, Rosie!" Fliss groaned, picking bits of paste out of her wig.

"Well, I didn't know!" I said defensively.

It was third time lucky. The next piece of wallpaper I cut and pasted was the right size. Kenny put it on the wall and Fliss smoothed it down, and the three of us stood back and admired it.

"OK, now we're really going for it!" Kenny announced confidently. "And the next piece, please!"

After that, we got on quite fast. We put up seven pieces of wallpaper and almost covered one long wall, so we were feeling pretty pleased with ourselves.

Then Fliss suddenly frowned. "That's funny…"

"What is?" I asked.

"Well, on the first piece we put up, the leaves on the flowers point downwards," Fliss said slowly. "And then on *that* piece, they point *upwards*, but on that one they point downwards again…"

"Kenny, you complete and total lamebrain!" I yelled. "You've put half the pieces on upside-down!"

"What? You're joking!" Kenny's mouth fell open.

Lyndz and Frankie were laughing their heads off across the room. "You'll have to peel them off, and do them again," Lyndz said between giggles.

"Nah, no-one'll notice—" Kenny began.

"Fliss already did!" I said pointedly. My heart sank as I looked at the upside-down wallpaper. It had taken ages to do, and now we were going to have to peel most of the pieces off again. You know what? I was definitely beginning to wonder if this had been such a good idea after all. Still, at least the painting was going OK. Lyndz and Frankie had finished the skirting-board on their side of the room, and were about to paint the radiator to match.

"Hey, Rosie, Lyndz and I thought we might try out some of the paint effects that they use in *Designer Rooms*," Frankie said. "What do you reckon?"

I cheered up a bit. "That sounds cool. What are you going to do?"

"We could try sponging," Lyndz suggested.

"No, spattering's better," said Frankie.

"What?" I said. I'd never heard of that one.

"Oh, it's pretty wicked." Frankie stuck her brush in the paint tin, and then aimed it at the radiator as we all gathered round. She flicked the brush smartly with her fingers, and specks of paint flew everywhere – and not just over the radiator either.

"Ow – my eye!" Lyndz shouted, clapping her hand over her face. "Frankie, you complete twit!"

"I think I *swallowed* some!" Fliss squealed in horror. "Is it poisonous?"

I glanced round at everyone. We all had very faint purple speckles all over our faces. We looked as though we had some horrible contagious disease.

"Spattering's *out*," I said firmly, and tried to grab the paintbrush off Frankie.

"Oh, don't be a wimp, Rosie!" Frankie retorted, an evil gleam in her eye as she avoided me and dunked the paintbrush in the tin again. "Look, it's great!" She deliberately flicked the paintbrush at the rest of us this time instead of at the radiator, and, again, paint flew everywhere.

"Yeah, you're right!" Lyndz said, scooping up some paint on her own brush. She aimed it at Frankie, and let fly. "It's great fun!"

"Aargh!" Frankie let out a yelp of protest as the paint spattered all over her face, and the rest of us burst out laughing.

"Right, you lot are dead!" Frankie announced, lunging towards the paint tin again.

"Oh, no you don't, Francesca Thomas!" Kenny shouted, rushing over to try and grab the brush from her. But she tripped over the flapping bottoms of her dungarees, and kicked the paint tin. The next second a thick stream of purple paint was flowing across the bare floorboards, and we were all paddling in it.

"Oh no!" I wailed, trying to get out of the way of the paint, and leaving purple footprints behind me. "Kenny, look what you've done!"

And right at that moment the bedroom door opened.

"What's going on?" My mum put her head in with a smile. "You're making an awful lot of—"

She stopped. I don't know what she noticed first. I guess it was probably the river of purple paint which was slopping round our ankles. But there were plenty of other things for her to look at. The upside-down wallpaper. The purple footprints. The paste in our hair and the paint spattered on our faces. Oh, and Fliss's wig…

We were in big trouble. And I mean BIG.

CHAPTER FOUR

"Rosie! Are you awake?"

"I am now!" I said crossly as Kenny poked me in the back. We'd had to move into Tiffany's bedroom last night, because my room wasn't in a fit state to sleep in. Me and Kenny were in Tiff's bed, and the others were in their sleeping-bags on the floor. "What time is it?"

"Seven o'clock." Kenny sat up and looked at her watch. "Do you reckon steam has stopped coming out of your mum's ears yet?"

"I wouldn't bet on it," I said grimly.

My mum's usually pretty laid back about

most things. But I'd never heard her shout as loudly as she did last night when she walked in on us doing the 'decorating'. It made my ears hurt just thinking about it.

Kenny stared at me, and started giggling. "You've still got purple paint on your face, and paste in your hair!"

"So've you!" I retorted. "You look like you've got the measles!"

"What are you two laughing about?" Frankie said sleepily. "You do realise that we're in doom *forever* after this?"

"Maybe our parents will see the funny side," Kenny suggested.

"What funny side?" Fliss demanded, sitting up in her sleeping-bag. "We're going to get *shredded*." Then she took one look at me and Kenny with our purple-spattered faces, and burst out laughing.

"See?" Kenny said hopefully.

The door opened then, and my mum looked in. "Time to get up, girls," she said very calmly and coolly, and went out again.

"I don't think your mum sees the funny

side, Rosie," said Lyndz. "Yuk! I've got paint in my fringe!"

"You should've worn a wig like me," Fliss remarked smugly, running a hand through her hair. She was the only one who hadn't got paste and paint in it.

"Did you see my mum's face when she clocked Fliss in that wig?" I said with a grin. "I thought she was going to faint!"

We all fell about laughing. We couldn't help it, even though we knew we were going to get it big-time.

We did. After breakfast, which we ate in silence, the others' parents started arriving to pick them up. The first to arrive was Frankie's mum. Straightaway my mum took her upstairs to show her what we'd done, and they stayed up there talking for about ten minutes. Meanwhile, we were all sitting in the living-room, nearly wetting ourselves. We weren't laughing *then*.

Frankie's mum didn't say much when she came back downstairs, but she looked pretty mad.

"Time to go, Francesca," was all she said. Frankie pulled a face at us – being called *Francesca* was not a good sign – and went. Lyndz's dad was next, and then Fliss's mum. Fliss was nearly crying by the time her mum came downstairs, and Mrs Sidebotham looked *really* angry, although that might have been because she'd got a smudge of purple paint on her posh jacket. Last of all was Dr McKenzie, Kenny's dad. As he was marching Kenny out of the door, his face grim, Kenny turned round, drew a finger across her throat and winked at me.

And that was that. Now I was left on my own with my mum.

"Well, Rosie?" She looked at me. "Have you got anything to say about all this?"

I stared down at my feet. "I wanted to have a nice bedroom, *just* for once," I muttered.

"And have you got one now?" My mum raised her eyebrows at me.

"No," I admitted.

"Exactly." My mum shook her head. "The room looks worse than when you started.

You've ruined all the paint and paper your dad bought, and half his tools."

"Well, if Dad had done it for me when he said he would, I wouldn't have tried to do it myself!" I retorted.

"Yes, well…" My mum's voice softened a bit, and I began to wonder hopefully if maybe we'd got away with it this time. "I blame your father as well, and I'm definitely going to have a word with him when he gets back from Majorca. But" – she'd started to sound angry again, which wasn't good – "you still shouldn't have done it. Do you realise how difficult it's going to be to get your room cleaned up?"

"Yes," I said dismally.

"Well, I've spoken to the other girls' parents," my mum went on, "and we've decided that instead of having a sleepover next week, the five of you can spend Friday evening and all day Saturday here, cleaning up the mess you made."

"OK," I agreed quickly. But there was more to come…

"And we've also decided that there'll be no

more sleepovers for a while—"

"*No more sleepovers*!" I gasped, outraged. "But, Mum—"

"No buts, Rosie!" My mum held up her hand. "There's not going to be another sleepover until you've proved to all of us that you won't do something as stupid as this ever again. Is that clear?"

I nodded miserably. No more sleepovers! How could we call ourselves the Sleepover Club if we couldn't even have a sleepover? This was the most gruesome thing which had ever happened to us! And in a way, it was all my fault. If I hadn't got so wound up about my bedroom being such a mess, none of this would have happened.

"Hey, Rosie! Have you got the measles or something?"

I gritted my teeth, and pushed my way past Ryan Scott and his stupid mate Danny McCloud into the school playground. It was Monday morning, and I still hadn't quite managed to get all the specks of paint off my face or out of my hair. I still had purple paint all over my hands too. I looked like something out of a horror film.

"Better keep away from her, Ryan!" I heard Danny McCloud shout. "You might catch something!"

"Oh, get a life!" I yelled crossly at the two sniggering idiots, but they just stood there laughing their heads off. I looked around for the others, but I couldn't see them. All I could see were the gruesome M&Ms and Alana Banana Palmer, giggling and pointing at me. You've *got* to remember the M&Ms, Emma Hughes and Emily Berryman. We call them the Queen and the Goblin because Emma's a snooty snob, and Emily's small, with a really gruff voice. They're so *sad*, it just isn't true. Alana Banana's sort of a friend of theirs too, but she's so dim, she doesn't bother us that much.

"Oh, how sweet!" said Emma Hughes sarcastically. "Look, Rosie's been learning how to paint!"

"You're in the wrong playground!" Emily

shouted at me. "This is the Juniors, the Infants is over there – that's where they do face-painting!"

"Oh, very funny!" I snapped.

"Maybe she'll learn how to use a knife and fork soon!" Emma trilled.

"And she won't have to wear nappies any more!" Emily added, and the two of them started roaring their heads off.

"What?" Alana Banana asked, looking puzzled. "I don't get it!"

I glared at them all and stomped off. I'd spotted Fliss, Kenny, Lyndz and Frankie sitting on a wall at the far end of the playground, their heads bent over a copy of *Cool!* magazine, and I hurried over to them. My mum hadn't let me phone any of the others yesterday, so I didn't know how they felt about not having any more sleepovers. I knew they'd be gutted. I just hoped they didn't blame me…

"Hi," I called, with a wave. Immediately Fliss rolled up the magazine and shoved it in her bag, and they all started shooting funny looks at each other.

"What's up with you lot?" I asked with a frown.

"Nothing," Frankie said quickly. Too quickly.

"Did your mum chew your ear off? Mine did."

"Yeah…" I looked round at Fliss, Kenny, Lyndz and Frankie suspiciously. There was definitely something odd going on. "Did your parents tell you we're not allowed to have any more sleepovers?"

They all nodded, and looked at each other again in a really strange way. I already felt pretty guilty, and that made me feel even worse.

"Why don't you just come right out and say it!" I shouted.

"Say what?" Fliss asked, trying to look innocent.

"You blame me!" I blurted out furiously. "You think it's my fault that we can't have any more sleepovers!"

I couldn't say anything else. I was so mad, I just turned round and walked off. No more sleepovers, and now it looked as if there was no more Sleepover Club as well…

CHAPTER FIVE

OK, I know I shouldn't have done that. But I was just so wound up, I couldn't help it. I *knew* the others blamed me for going on and on about my bedroom, and getting them all involved. And I did feel guilty about it. But they were supposed to be my friends, weren't they? We should all stick together.

I was so upset that when we went into class, I even asked our teacher, Mrs Weaver, if I could sit on a different table. Mrs Weaver did a bit of a double-take when she noticed my purple face, but she told me I could sit on Ryan Scott and Danny McCloud's table. Great. That was only just about better than sitting with the M&Ms and dozy Alana Banana.

The others started whispering and pointing when I took my stuff and sat down on another table, but I didn't look at them. I thought they might come over and try to talk to me, but we were supposed to be reading in silence before assembly so I guess they couldn't. Still, I thought crossly, if they *really* wanted to make it up with me, they could pass me a note.

The first note that came was from Kenny. It said: "*Don't be such a sad dork, Rosie! We don't blame you, you lemon! What did you go and throw a fit like that for?*"

The second note was from Lyndz. She dropped it on my lap when she went over to the bookcase to change her book. It said: "*Sorry, Rosie! We were only being a bit funny this morning because we were planning a surprise for you – watch out for Frankie's note!*"

Frankie's note said: "*There's a competition in Fliss's Cool! magazine to win a bedroom makeover!!! That's what we were looking at when you arrived this morning! Fliss'll tell you about it!"*

Fliss wrote: *"We were going to enter the competition for you, but we weren't going to say anything, in case we didn't win. The closing date for the comp is tomorrow, so we've got to do it TODAY!!!"*

I could hardly believe it. A competition to win a bedroom makeover? That first prize just *had* to have my name on it! I looked across the classroom at the others, grinned at them and gave them a double thumbs-up. Then I put my hand in the air, and waved it about until I got Mrs Weaver's attention.

"Yes, Rosie?" she asked, looking up from the maths books she was marking.

"Miss, can I go back to my old table?" I asked eagerly.

"I suppose so." Mrs Weaver looked at me over the top of her glasses. "But before you do, could you put all those notes that Frankie, Laura, Lyndsey and Felicity have been passing to you in the wastepaper basket?"

I turned pink, and glanced at the others. That's the trouble with Mrs Weaver. She's got X-ray vision.

"Thank you, Rosie," Mrs Weaver went on coolly when I'd chucked the notes away. "And thanks, all of you girls, for volunteering to give up your lunch hour and stay in to tidy the library."

I squirmed a bit, but I guess we'd got off pretty lightly. And I was friends with the others again, so it was worth it! Just then the bell went for assembly, and everyone rushed to put their books away, so under cover of the noise I dashed over to them.

"Sorry!" I said breathlessly, and Kenny thumped me on the back.

"Welcome back, Prune-face!" she said.

"Here!" Fliss thrust the copy of *Cool!* magazine under my nose, and I had a quick look at it.

"It says here you have to explain in no more than 80 words why you should get a bedroom makeover!" I looked round at the others in dismay. "I'm useless at this sort of competition – I can never think what to say!"

"Ah, but we're going to help you!" Frankie told me with a grin.

"Yeah, we're going to make sure you win!" Kenny chimed in.

"The other entrants won't stand a chance against the Sleepover Club!" Fliss boasted.

"It's in the bag!" Lyndz added.

"Er – thanks, guys," I said. "But if it's got to be done today, *when* are we going to do it?"

"We'll have a bit of time after school before the last post goes," Lyndz suggested, but Frankie shook her head.

"We need longer than that. What about lunchtime?"

"We're tidying the library, remember?" the rest of us said gloomily.

"Well, we'll just have to try and do both!" Frankie said in a determined voice. "We can't miss this chance to get Rosie's bedroom looking good – and if we win, it might just stop our parents having a go at us! And then we might get our sleepovers back too..."

*　　*　　*

"Look at this!" Fliss wailed, as we all hurried into the school library straight after we'd finished our lunch. "It's a complete tip!"

"It looks like someone's been having a book fight!" Kenny said, gazing round. There were books lying all over the chairs and tables, and on the floor too. My heart sank. It was going to take us ages to clear up this mess. How on earth could we write my competition entry and get everything tidied up before the afternoon bell?

"Hey, I've had a fabbo idea for the comp!" Frankie announced suddenly. "Why don't we send a poem?"

"Oh, yeah, right!" I said. "I can't write poems, dumbo!"

"No, but I can!" Frankie pointed out, and my face split into a big grin. Frankie was right. She was *excellent* at English.

"Good one, Franks!" Kenny agreed eagerly. "Look, you'd better sit down and write it, while the rest of us get on with the tidying-up."

"OK." Frankie looked at Fliss. "Have you got

the magazine?"

Fliss shook her head. "I left it in the classroom. D'you want me to go and get it?"

Before Frankie could reply, the door opened, and Mrs Weaver popped her head in. "How are we getting on?" she asked briskly. "Oh, dear, not very well. Still, there's always tomorrow lunchtime as well…"

"Don't worry, Miss, we'll finish it today!" Kenny broke in hastily. She picked up the nearest pile of books, but they were too heavy for her and she ended up dropping most of them on the carpet. Mrs Weaver sighed, and went out.

"Do you want me to go and get the mag?" Fliss asked Frankie again.

Frankie shook her head. "Better not," she said. "If Weaver catches you, she'll go ballistic. Rosie can fill in the entry form later."

"Come on, get a move on!" Kenny said to the rest of us as Frankie sat down. "Or we'll be stuck in here tomorrow too!"

"Stop bossing us around, Kenny!" Fliss

sniffed, and Frankie glared at us.

"Do you mind? I'm trying to write a prize-winning poem here!"

So we tiptoed around, putting the books away and tidying up the shelves while Frankie got down to work. We were pretty quiet, except when Fliss accidentally dropped an encyclopaedia on Lyndz's toe, but as time went by, I was really starting to get worried. It was nearly time for the bell, and Frankie hadn't said a word for about forty-five minutes.

"OK!" Frankie threw her pen down just as the bell rang for the end of lunchtime, and Kenny put the last book away on the shelf. "I've done it!"

"Excellent!" I said, and we all rushed over.

"Go on, Frankie, read it," said Fliss.

Frankie cleared her throat and read:

"My bedroom's a tip,
It has to be said,
All that I've got
Is a wardrobe and bed!

There's paperless walls
And carpetless floor,
It's really a dump,
I can stand it no more.

I need a cool room
For my friends to sleep over,
I'd so love the prize
Of a bedroom makeover!"

"That's excellent!" Lyndz said admiringly, and we all nodded.

"I reckon I've got a great chance of winning with that!" I said breathlessly. "Thanks, Frankie!"

Frankie shrugged. "I guess some people have got it – and some people haven't!"

"What, a big head, you mean?" Kenny said teasingly, and Frankie thumped her.

"Come on, we're going to be late back to class," Lyndz said, pulling open the library door. "Haven't we got Art this afternoon?"

"Oh, brill – painting! My best thing!" Frankie said, pulling a face, and we all started giggling.

When we finally made it back to class, Mrs Weaver had already taken the register, and everyone was moving around collecting their paints and brushes, and putting newspaper down on their tabletops.

"All finished, girls?" Mrs Weaver called to us, and we nodded virtuously.

"I'll cut out the entry form from the magazine, and Rosie can fill it in," Fliss told us in a low voice, as we went over to our table. Then she gave a little scream, and grabbed my arm really tightly.

"Ow!" I gasped, trying to pull myself free. "What's up with you?"

"I left the magazine on the table!" Fliss wailed dramatically. "And now it's *gone!*"

CHAPTER SIX

We all stood there with our mouths open, staring down at the table as if the magazine would suddenly appear out of thin air.

"What do you mean, it's gone?" Kenny hissed at Fliss.

"Which part of that sentence didn't you understand, Kenny?" Fliss snapped back. "The magazine isn't here!"

"It must be here *somewhere*," Lyndz said, getting down on her knees to look under the table. But it wasn't there either.

"We've got to have that magazine!" I said urgently. "We can't enter the competition without the entry form!"

"Oh no!" said Fliss suddenly in a horrified voice.

"What?" we all said together.

"I don't believe it!" Fliss said, sounding really choked.

"WHAT?" we all said again.

Fliss didn't answer. Instead she rushed across the room towards the M&Ms' table. Emma Hughes and Emily Berryman were over the other side, collecting their paints, and the only person there was Alana Banana Palmer, who was mixing up some colours and trying them out on the newspaper spread over her table.

"Look!" Fliss said, pointing with a shaky finger.

At first I couldn't see what Fliss was going on about. Then I took a closer look. Alana's side of the table wasn't just covered with old newspaper, it was also covered with pages from a magazine. 'Win a bedroom makeover!' leapt out at me from one of the pages, which was covered with big black, orange and green

58

blotches, where Alana had been trying out her colours.

"It's the magazine!" I yelled. I leapt forward, and dragged the pages off the table, nearly knocking over the pot of water.

"Hey, what's the matter with you?" Alana asked, looking dozily from me to Fliss.

"That's my magazine, you birdbrain!" Fliss snapped. "Who said you could nick it to cover your stupid table?"

Alana shrugged. "Oh, it was just lying there, so I took it. I didn't think you'd mind."

"Well, I do!" Fliss retorted angrily.

"And so do I!" I added, glaring at Alana, but it was like water off a duck's back.

"Sorry," Alana said dreamily, and went back to mixing her paints.

"Can we use the entry form or not?" Kenny asked me urgently.

"Not unless we think big black and orange splodges all over it are going to impress the judges!" I said miserably. I showed the competition page to the others. Alana Banana had really gone to town on it. You couldn't even *see* most of the entry form because of the paint all over it.

"You don't think the M&Ms set this up, do you?" Fliss asked suspiciously.

"No, I don't reckon so." Kenny glanced over at the M&Ms, who weren't taking any notice of us or Alana. They were talking to Ryan and Danny over by the paints cupboard. "Not this time. They'd be over here like a shot having a good laugh if they had."

"The M&Ms don't even know we want to enter the competition anyway," Lyndz added. "It's all down to Alana Banana being a dozy twit!"

"All right, don't panic!" said Frankie. "We'll just have to nip along to the newsagent's after school, and get another copy. Simple!"

We all heaved a sigh of relief. Except Fliss.

"There might not be any left," she pointed out, "The new edition of the mag comes out tomorrow."

"We'll just have to risk it," I said anxiously. I couldn't see what else we could do, even though it was a bit dodgy leaving it all to the last minute.

"We'd better get our painting stuff," Lyndz whispered. "Mrs Weaver's giving us dirty looks."

We all trailed over to the paints cupboard, and collected our equipment. Everybody looked pretty down, and I felt really frustrated. Without a form, I didn't have a hope of even entering the competition, let alone winning it. At that moment, I could have picked up the pot of dirty water on Alana's table and poured it over her head!

Kenny had gone to get us some aprons, and she was last to get back to our table. She chucked the aprons down, and grinned round at us.

"Guess what? I think I've found another copy of the magazine!"

"What!" I didn't believe her at first – I was sure she was having us on. "Where?"

"Take a look over there, on the cupboard!" Kenny nodded across the classroom. "It's the magazine all right! There's just one tiny little problem…"

We all looked where Kenny had indicated. Someone's bag was sitting on one of the cupboards, and poking out of the top was a rolled-up copy of *Cool!* magazine.

"Hey, Kenny's right!" I gasped. "Do you think they'll give me the entry form, whoever it is?"

"I can't see it somehow," Frankie said, pulling a face. "That's Emma Hughes's bag!"

"Yeah," said Kenny. "That's the tiny little problem I mentioned."

"Oh no!" My heart fell right down into my shoes with a loud THUD. The magazine *would* have to belong to Emma Hughes!

"Yeah, she's the only one in the class who's got a prissy pink rucksack like that," Kenny went on.

Fliss glared at her. "*I've* got a pink rucksack, Kenny!"

"Yeah, but yours is much nicer!" Kenny said quickly, and turned to Frankie. "What d'you reckon, Franks? Shall I have a go at nicking it or what?"

"No!" Fliss looked scared to death. "What if

you get caught? Mrs Weaver will skin you alive!"

"She's right, Kenny," Lyndz chimed in. "It's too risky."

"Yeah, I agree." Frankie thought for a moment or two. "I reckon the only thing we can do is ask Emma to give it to us."

"Oh yeah, I can see that happening right off!" Kenny scoffed. "Like the Queen's *really* going to hand it over just like that!"

"I didn't mean that," Frankie said in a crushing tone, "I meant we could buy it off her."

"What? No way!" Kenny gasped. "We'd never hear the end of it!"

"Well, have you got a better idea?" Frankie asked.

"Yeah, I told you," Kenny said impatiently. "I'll go over there and nick it when she's not looking!"

"NO!" the rest of us said together.

"Fine!" Kenny snapped. "Well, if you want to let the M&Ms get one over on us…"

We all looked at each other, and I felt really

bad. It was all my fault that we had to go crawling to the M&Ms. Well, it was my dad's fault really…

"Anyway," Kenny went on, "I bet Emma won't sell it to you – you know what she's like!"

"We'll have to try," Lyndz said.

Fliss groaned. "Emma's going to *love* this!"

"I'd better be the one to ask her," I said quickly, "because it's me who needs the entry form." I wasn't looking forward to being nice to Emma Hughes one bit, but I knew I couldn't expect the others to do it. I took my purse out of my pocket, and counted out 90p, which is what the magazine cost.

"I don't mind asking her—" Kenny began, but Frankie shook her head.

"Nah, you and Emma would be fighting in one second flat! It's best if Rosie does it."

"OK, but we're all going with her," Kenny said in a determined voice.

"Don't say anything to Emma about why we want the magazine," Frankie warned me, and I nodded.

Mrs Weaver was busy over by the sink at that moment, so it was a good time for all of us to leg it across the classroom to the M&Ms' table. Emma Hughes and Emily Berryman looked suspiciously at us as we stopped in front of them, although Alana was too busy painting to take any notice.

"Look what the cat dragged in, Emily!" Emma sniffed.

"Why don't you try zipping your big fat mouth—" Kenny began crossly, but she was bundled back across the room by Frankie and Lyndz, leaving me and Fliss to negotiate with Emma Hughes.

"Look, is that your magazine there?" I asked quickly, pointing at the pink rucksack just behind her.

Emma looked even more suspicious, as if I'd asked her a trick question. "What do you mean?"

"I just want to know, because if it is, I want to buy it," I said in a rush.

The M&Ms looked at each other in disbelief. "Why?" Emily Berryman asked, puzzled.

"I just want it." I held out my hand, and showed them the 90p. "Here's the money."

Emma and Emily looked at the money, smirked at each other and then turned away and went into a little huddle. They were muttering together, but I couldn't hear what they were saying. Then Emma grinned at me. It was a pretty evil grin, so I guessed it wasn't going to be good news.

"Yeah, you can have it," she said.

"Oh, thanks, Emma!" I said, surprised.

"But it'll cost you five pounds!"

"*Five pounds?*" Fliss squealed. "But it's only 90p!"

"That's my final offer," Emma Hughes said smugly while Emily Berryman sniggered away in the background. "Take it or leave it!"

Fliss and I hurried back to our table to tell the others.

"*Five pounds!*" Kenny repeated, her eyes wide. "What a slimeball! I *told* you I should have nicked it!"

"We'd better pool all our dosh and see how much we've got," Frankie suggested. So we all emptied out our purses and pockets, and put the money on the table. We had £3.15.

"D'you think they'll take it?" Fliss asked doubtfully.

"I'll give it a go," I said. I scooped the money up and went back across the room. The M&Ms started giggling and nudging each other as soon as they saw me coming.

"We've only got £3.15," I said to Emma Hughes.

Emma sniffed. "Well, I suppose that'll have to do!" She leaned over and took the magazine out of her rucksack, and I gave her the money. "Nice doing business with you!" she called after me, sounding really self-satisfied as I went back across the room. Then she and Emily started sniggering again. But this time I didn't care about Emma getting one over on us – I'd got the magazine! That was all that mattered.

"Quick, Rosie, fill in the entry form, and then we can post it after school!" Frankie said urgently.

I flipped quickly through the magazine,

looking for the competition page. But when I found it I got a big shock.

"Oh no!" I gasped.

"What?" The others crowded round me

The competition page was there all right, with its headline 'Win a bedroom makeover!', but there was a big empty space where the entry form should have been!

Kenny grabbed the magazine from me, and stuck her fist through the hole in the page. "Someone's already cut the form out!" she gasped.

"Emma must be entering the competition herself!" Lyndz said gloomily.

"That girl gets right up my nose!" Kenny clenched her fists and glared across the classroom at Emma. "The one thing we want in the stupid magazine – and she goes and cuts it out!"

"At least she doesn't know why we wanted to buy the magazine," Fliss pointed out. "So we won't have to listen to her and the Goblin going on about how they tricked us!"

"No, they'd be killing themselves laughing if

they knew!" I added miserably.

"So what do we do now?" Lyndz asked.

We all looked at each other.

"We're going to have to go to the news-agent's after school, and hope and pray that they've got a copy of the magazine left!" Frankie said grimly.

CHAPTER SEVEN

"Come on, Fliss!" Kenny yelled impatiently over her shoulder. "Put some effort into it – stop running like a girl!"

"I *am* a girl!" Fliss yelled back crossly, hurrying to catch the rest of us up. "Why do we have to run anyway? The newsagent's doesn't close till six!"

"Yeah, but the last post goes at five o'clock!" I pointed out, "and we've got to fill in the entry form yet."

We'd charged out of school so fast when the home bell went, we'd almost knocked everyone else over. The M&Ms had been all set to come over and gloat about how they'd made us pay more than three times what the magazine cost, but we'd left them standing. Now we were heading down the High Street in the pouring rain towards the biggest newsagent's in Cuddington.

"Here we are!" Frankie skidded to a halt outside the shop.

"Quick, inside!" Kenny yelled, yanking the door open and pushing us all in.

We all dived in, and the shop assistant behind the till looked a bit alarmed. We ignored her though, and dashed over to the shelves of magazines.

"It's not here!" Fliss squeaked despairingly, as we scanned all the racks.

"Look behind the other kids' magazines!" I said urgently. "Sometimes they get covered up, especially if there's not many copies left."

We all started lifting up the magazines and looking underneath them, but nothing. And then—

"I've got it!" I shouted, waving the magazine over my head, "I've got it – the very last copy!"

"Yes!" Kenny held up her hand, and I gave her a high five.

"Check it first before you buy it," Lyndz said with a grin. "Just in case the shop assistant's decided to enter the comp, and cut the form out!"

The shop assistant was staring at us now as if we were completely off our heads, but I didn't care. I had a quick look through the mag, and there was the entry form safe and sound.

"Result!" I said, beaming round at the others. "Someone'll have to lend me some money to buy it though. I gave all mine to Emma Hughes."

There was a sudden, rather horrible silence.

"I gave all mine to Emma too," said Fliss slowly.

"And me," said Kenny and Lyndz together.

"So did I," Frankie added, looking a bit sick.

"Are you telling me," I said in a very calm, very cool voice, "that *none of us* has got any money?"

The others nodded miserably.

"Oh NO!" I wailed. "What are we going to do?"

"My place is closest, so you lot wait here, and I'll nip home and get some dosh," Kenny suggested. "I'll even break open Molly the Monster's piggy-bank if I have to!"

"If you're not going to buy that magazine, can you put it back please?" said the shop assistant sharply.

Reluctantly I put the magazine back, hiding it behind a copy of the *Beano*. Lyndz nudged me.

"We'd better wait outside," she muttered. "I don't think that shop assistant likes us very much!"

"I'll be as quick as I can," Kenny said as we all went over to the door.

We were just about to barge through when Sally Peters came in. She goes to our school, but she's only in Year 3 so we don't know her that well. She went over to the shelves of magazines, and, as we rushed out of the door, I turned round, just to check that she wasn't after my copy of *Cool!* I nearly dropped down dead with shock. Sally Peters had *my magazine* in her hand, and she was paying the shop assistant for it! I groaned loudly.

"Don't bother going home, Kenny!" I grabbed her sleeve just as she was about to take off like a rocket. "There's no point!"

"Why not?" Kenny asked.

"Because Sally Peters has just bought it!" This really wasn't my day.

"No!" Kenny, Fliss, Frankie and Lyndz all immediately pressed their noses right against the window and stared in, almost giving the assistant a heart attack.

"Rosie's right – she's bought it!" Fliss said tragically.

"Well, we'll just have to get it off her somehow, won't we?" Kenny retorted in a determined voice, as Sally came out of the shop with the magazine in her hand.

"No violence, Kenny!" Frankie warned her. I think she was only half-joking as well!

"Hi, Sal!" Kenny said in a super-friendly voice. Sally looked a bit alarmed, which was probably because Kenny had never spoken to her before. "All right?"

"Yes, thank you," Sally said cautiously.

"Well, we were wondering if you could do us a favour," Kenny went on, grinning at her. "You see, we really need that magazine you've got there, so—"

Sally's bottom lip began to tremble. "If you start picking on me, I'll tell my teacher!"

"Kenny, you're frightening the blinking life out of her!" I hissed, pushing her aside. "Get out of the way and let me handle this!"

"I was only trying to be nice!" Kenny said in an injured tone.

"Look, Sally," I said politely, "We're not trying to bully you, but we really need that magazine. We'll give you two quid for it."

Sally shook her head, and clutched the magazine more firmly. "No, thanks."

I was beginning to get desperate now. "OK, Sally, we'll give you anything you want if you'll let us have that magazine!"

"Except my new Leicester City shirt," Kenny added.

Sally looked a bit more interested. "Did you say *anything*?"

"Yeah, anything." I hoped she wouldn't ask for a pony or a computer or something outrageous like that. "What do you say?"

Sally was staring at Fliss's pink rucksack very intently. "I like that keyring," she announced, pointing at the big purple and white plastic flower which hung from one of the straps.

"What keyring?" Fliss asked sharply. Then her face dropped. "Oh no, not mine! I only bought it last week!"

We all stared hard at Fliss. We didn't even have to say anything.

"Oh, all right!" Fliss said in a bad-tempered voice. She undid the keyring and handed it to Sally, who gave me the magazine.

"At last!" I said triumphantly, as Sally began to fasten the keyring to her bag, beaming all over her face. "I'm not going to let this magazine out of my sight now until I've posted my competition entry!"

Trust me to go and open my big mouth.

When I glanced up the street, the next thing I saw was two boys on mountain bikes charging along the pavement straight towards us.

"Look at those idiots riding on the pavement!" I said angrily. "They're going to knock someone over!"

There was an old lady with a walking-stick coming slowly towards us. Instead of riding into the road to avoid her, the two boys stayed on the pavement, and swerved round her. The old lady, who hadn't heard them behind her, was startled and almost fell. She clutched at her heart and looked like she couldn't breathe for a moment.

"You prats!" Kenny yelled crossly. She was just about to hurry over to the old lady to see if she was all right, when we realised that the two boys were pedalling straight towards us, grinning all over their faces!

"Get out of the way!" Frankie yelled at the rest of us, yanking Lyndz and Sally into the shop doorway. Fliss and I both tried to jump back too, but we panicked, and bumped into each other really hard. The magazine flew out of my hand, and landed with a splash in the wet gutter…

CHAPTER EIGHT

"My magazine!" I yelled, lunging forward.

I would've got flattened by the two boys on the bikes, but Kenny had refused to move off the pavement, and had stood her ground. The two boys had got a bit spooked by that, and had braked to a halt so fast they'd nearly flown head-over-heels over their handlebars. So I was able to dash over to the gutter and retrieve the magazine. It was *soaking* wet.

"What do you think you two saddoes are doing, riding on the pavement!" Kenny shouted at the two boys. "Don't you know what the road's for?"

"Oh, shut up!" said one of the boys with a grin. They were a bit older than us, but not much, and they were wearing the Cuddington Comprehensive uniform. "We were just having a laugh, that's all!"

"Well, we're not laughing and neither is that lady back there!" Lyndz told them furiously, as Frankie went over to check that the old lady was all right.

"Haven't you got a brain between you!" Fliss yelled at them, taking the sopping magazine from me and holding it by one corner. "Look what you've done to our magazine, you wallies!"

That was pretty radical for Fliss to start having a go at a couple of boys! There were quite a few people in the street now, and they were all looking curiously in our direction.

"So what?" sneered the other boy, but he looked a bit alarmed when Kenny stormed over to him and grabbed his handlebars.

"Since when have you been so hard, Michael Johnson? I remember you crying when you lost the sack race at Sports Day!"

Michael turned bright pink. "Come on, Rick, let's get out of here," he muttered, and they rode off. But this time they moved off the pavement and on to the road.

"Do you know them?" I asked Kenny.

"Oh, they used to be at our school before you came – they left last year," Kenny explained as Frankie hurried back over to us.

"They're OK, really, just kind of brain-dead!"

"The old lady's all right," Frankie said. "She's a bit shaken, that's all."

"That's good." Dismally I looked down at the magazine which Fliss was still holding. "But what are we supposed to do now? The magazine's ruined!"

"No, it isn't," Lyndz chimed in. "We can dry it out, can't we?"

"Sure we can!" Kenny agreed. "We'll go round to my house – come on!"

I glanced at my watch. "But it's ten past four – we'll never make the last post!"

"Try looking on the bright side for once, Rosie!" Kenny said, giving me a shove. "Let's go!"

We all ran the short distance to Kenny's house as if we were in training for the Olympics. As soon as we got there, we all hurried upstairs to Kenny's bedroom, and she laid the magazine, open at the competition page, down on the hot radiator.

"It shouldn't take long," Kenny said optimistically, as we all pulled off our wet jackets. "We've still got plenty of time before the post goes."

I wasn't so sure. But there was nothing I could do about it, except wait.

"Oh no, it's the Purple Posse!" Kenny's older sister Molly, who shared the bedroom, came in, grinning hugely, and dumped her schoolbag on her bed. She looked at our still faintly purple-speckled faces, and began to snigger. "Very nice – but I don't think it'll catch on!"

"Why don't you go and do something useful, Molly?" Kenny suggested. "Like falling down the stairs?"

"This room's half mine, remember!" Molly stood irritatingly in the doorway with her arms folded. "And I don't want your smelly little friends going on my side of it!"

"Don't worry, we won't," Frankie said scathingly. "We wouldn't want to catch anything!"

"Looks like you already have – the Purple Plague!" Molly the Monster retorted, roaring with laughter at her own pathetic joke.

Kenny reached over and kicked the door shut. The last thing we heard was Molly thundering downstairs shouting, "Mum! Kenny's being a pain!"

"That's got rid of her!" Kenny said with satisfaction. She went over and picked up the magazine, but the paper was still far too wet to write on. "Oh, well, it won't be much longer…"

We all sat in silence, looking at the magazine on the radiator, and at the clock on the wall. Time ticked by. It wasn't until nearly twenty to five that the magazine was dry enough for me to fill in my name and address on the entry form, and then copy Frankie's poem on to it. The paper was a bit wrinkled and a bit yellowed, but it wasn't too bad.

"Come on, Rosie, hurry up!" Fliss kept saying, which was putting me off no end. I made about a million mistakes, but at last it was finished.

"It's nearly five to five," Lyndz said in a worried voice. "Are we going to make it?"

"Get your coats on, and stop babbling!" Kenny ordered, stuffing the entry form into an envelope that she'd nicked from her dad's study and scribbling an address on it. "Leave your bags here, they'll only slow us down. You can come back for them afterwards."

We all grabbed our coats and dashed for the door. As we raced for the stairs, Molly the Monster was coming along the landing.

"Oh, you're going – good!" she said, blocking our way.

"Move it, Molly!" Kenny yelled, trying to push past her.

"Why should I?" Molly asked in an infuriatingly smug voice. "I was here first!"

We all looked at each other, and then we just charged past her. We didn't exactly knock her over, but as we disappeared down the stairs, we heard her yelling "MUM!" again.

"We've really got to run now!" I gasped as Kenny yanked open the front door. "It's four minutes to five o'clock!"

We belted down the road in the direction of the nearest postbox. I was trying to calculate how far away it was. I wasn't sure, but it had to be at least five minutes' walk. OK, we were running, but would we make it?

We got to the postbox just as the van pulled up alongside it, and Kenny quickly stuffed the envelope through the slot. Everyone started cheering and whooping. We all stood around as the postie emptied the box, just to make sure he didn't leave our letter behind, although he gave us a few funny looks. Then, as he slung the sack in the back of his van and drove off, we all breathed a large sigh of relief.

"OK, back to mine for chocolate biscuits and Coke to celebrate!" Kenny yelled, slapping me on the back. We all went off down the road – and then suddenly realised that there were only four of us. Frankie was still standing by the postbox, a look of horror on her face.

"Kenny, what address did you put on the envelope?" she asked slowly.

"Kenny, you didn't put the wrong address on it, did you?" I chimed in, alarmed.

"No, I didn't!" Kenny defended herself. "I put the magazine's address in London."

"I *thought* I saw London on the envelope!" Frankie wailed. "That wasn't the right address! The address for the competition entries was somewhere in Nottingham!"

CHAPTER NINE

"Maybe the magazine will send it on," Kenny said hopefully, as we walked slowly back to her house. "It'll only be a day late."

"I think they're pretty strict about the closing date," Frankie said gloomily. "They'll probably just throw away any entries that arrive late!"

"Just my luck!" I muttered. I was tired out, I was broke, I was wet and I was miserable. And I still had a gruesome bedroom...

"Sorry, Rosie." Kenny slung an arm round my shoulders. "Maybe your dad'll get his act together when he comes back from holiday."

"He's more likely to have a go at me because we ruined all the paint and wallpaper he bought," I muttered. "And what's going to happen about our sleepovers now?"

We walked the rest of the way back to Kenny's house to collect our bags in gloomy silence. As Kenny unlocked the door, and we all trooped miserably into the hall, Molly the Monster popped out of the living-room, grinning all over her ugly face.

"Dad's looking for you, Laura!" she announced gleefully. "*And* your little friends too! What have you done now?"

"Dad!" Kenny looked worried. "What's he doing home at this time?"

"He finished his house calls early," Molly said smugly. "And now he wants a word with you!"

Kenny stuck her tongue out at Molly, and turned to the rest of us. "Oh no! Can anything else go wrong today?"

"What do you think your dad wants, Kenny?" Fliss asked nervously.

Kenny shrugged. "Who knows?"

"Ah, Kenny." Dr McKenzie came out of the study, and we all looked at him anxiously. He didn't *look* too angry, but parents are like that sometimes. They pretend to be all cool, and then they hit you with it. "I want a word with you – and the other girls."

We all shuffled into the study. It felt a bit like being sent to the headmistress's office at school, because Dr McKenzie sat down at the desk, and we all stood in a line in front of him. I was starting to get seriously worried. What if our parents had decided that not only were we not allowed to have any sleepovers, we also weren't allowed to see each other out of school, or something gruesome like that?

"Well," said Dr McKenzie, but he didn't get the chance to say any more, because just then the telephone rang. I glanced along at the others. Fliss looked as if her knees were knocking together, and even Kenny looked a bit sick.

"Yes, hello, Mrs Dixon," said Dr McKenzie. "Yes, yes, I know. Yes, I will. Thank you for calling. Goodbye." He put the phone down and looked at us. "That was the sixth phone call I've had in the last twenty minutes," he said. "They were all from people who were in the High Street this afternoon."

We looked at each other, puzzled. What was going on?

"Apparently you girls stood up to some boys who were cycling on the pavement, and impressed a lot of people who were watching!" Dr McKenzie smiled at us, and we all nearly collapsed with relief. "You helped an old lady who nearly got knocked over too, didn't you?"

We all nodded dumbly. We were too surprised to say anything.

"Well, she's called Mrs Grahame and she's one of my patients," Dr McKenzie went on. "She called me too. Said you were all a credit to your parents!"

We grinned at each other.

"I wouldn't mind betting your mums and dads have had a few calls too." And Dr McKenzie glanced at me, Fliss, Lyndz and Frankie.

"See, Dad?" Kenny said proudly, "We don't mess up *all* the time!"

"I'm glad to hear it," her father said with a twinkle in his eye.

"So can we have our sleepovers back?" Kenny asked.

"Don't push it, Laura." Dr McKenzie reached for the phone again. "I'll think about it. Now off you go, I've got a few calls to make."

We all piled out of the study, chattering excitedly.

"I reckon we're back in!" Kenny muttered in a low voice. "Our parents are going to be dead pleased now – they love it when other people think we're cool!"

"D'you really think so?" I asked eagerly.

"You bet!" said Frankie. "Kenny's right – I think we'll get our sleepovers back double-quick!"

"Not this week-end though," Lyndz pointed out. "We've still got to clean up Rosie's bedroom!"

* * *

"Wow! This looks gruesome!" Frankie muttered, as I flung open the door to my bedroom and let everyone in. "It looks even worse than I remember!"

"Mind the paint," I said, pointing at the floor. "Some of it's still a bit sticky."

It was Friday evening. Everyone had come over to my house and changed into old clothes to start cleaning up the mess. There was no way we would finish it tonight though – it was probably going to take us most of the week-end. Still, our parents had been so pleased with all the phone calls they got from the people in the High Street, telling them how wonderful we were for standing up to those boys, that they'd decided to lift the sleepover ban. So we were all pretty happy, even though we wouldn't have time for a sleepover that week-end.

"Well, I reckon that wallpaper looks OK," Kenny said, squinting at it. "You can hardly even notice that some of the pieces are upside-down!"

"Sorry," I said, grabbing a piece that wasn't

stuck down properly and beginning to peel it away from the wall. "Every single bit has got to come off!"

"Hello, girls." My mum popped her head round the door, and grinned at us. "Have you made a start yet?"

"Not yet," I said.

"Well, have you got room for a few more helpers?" she asked, and opened the door wide. We could hardly believe our eyes as in came Frankie's mum and dad, Kenny's mum, Lyndz's dad and Fliss's mum, all wearing old clothes and smiling at us.

"What's— what's going on?" I gasped.

"Well, we thought that you deserved a bit of help, after you were all so heroic last Monday!" said Frankie's mum.

"Yes, but I don't know much about DIY!" said Fliss's mum anxiously. "So you'll have to give me something easy to do!"

"Hm, this is a bit of a mess!" said Lyndz's dad, looking round with a practised eye. "But we'll soon get it cleared up."

"There's something else..." my mum said,

looking at me. "We're not just going to clean up the mess – everyone's kindly offered to help us decorate it too!"

"What?" I blinked, not quite believing my ears.

"We're going to get your room done once and for all!" My mum gave me a hug. "If we all work really hard, we might be able to get it finished this week-end too."

"Do you *mean* it?" My legs went all wobbly then, and I had to sit down on the bed. The others cheered loudly, and rushed over to thump me on the back.

"Excellent!" said Kenny. "Don't let my mum do anything too difficult though – she's hopeless at DIY!"

"What a cheek!" said Mrs McKenzie indignantly. "At least I wouldn't have put the wallpaper on upside-down!"

"Thanks, Mum and Dad!" Frankie said gratefully. "But what about the baby?"

"I don't think the baby's going to mind if I do a bit of painting!" Mrs Thomas said. "Come on, let's get started."

Lyndz's dad was already scraping the sticky paint off the floorboards, and getting Mrs Sidebotham to do the same. Fliss's mum, who was wearing a completely spotless pair of white dungarees and a pink tee-shirt, looked as if she'd rather be anywhere but here, but she was doing her best.

"We're going to need some more wallpaper and paint," my mum said as we began to strip the wall. "Do you want the same again, Rosie, or do you want to choose something new?"

I shook my head. I'd just had a really *radical* idea. "*I* don't want to choose it," I said. "I want *them* to!" And I pointed at Lyndz, Kenny, Frankie and Fliss, who all turned and stared at me.

"What are you going on about?" Frankie asked.

"I want you lot to design my bedroom for me!" I gabbled excitedly. "I want you to choose the wallpaper and the paint and all that – and I won't see it till it's finished! It'll be just like *Designer Rooms*!"

The others grinned at me.

"Awesome!" Kenny exclaimed. "That's an excellent idea!"

"Are you sure, Rosie?" Fliss asked a bit doubtfully. "What if you don't like it?"

"Yeah, remember some of the people on *Designer Rooms* throw a fit when they see their house again!" Lyndz added.

"I trust you!" I said. "I know you'll do a great job!"

"I've got some brill ideas already!" Kenny began, but Frankie elbowed her in the ribs. "We're not having anything to do with football!" she said, and Kenny's face fell.

"Hey, we ought to get on with designing it right now!" Frankie suggested, dropping the cloth she was using to mop up the spilt paint. "Come on, you lot!"

"Hey, where are you going?" called Frankie's dad, as Frankie, Kenny, Fliss and Lyndz all bolted for the door. "Trust you to disappear when there's work to be done!"

"Sorry, Dad!" Frankie called back over her shoulder. "We've got something much more important to do!"

I grinned to myself. I couldn't wait to see my new bedroom – and I knew the Sleepover Club wouldn't let me down!

CHAPTER TEN

Everything was so exciting, it was like being on the real *Designer Rooms*! For a start, Frankie and the others wouldn't let me even get a *sniff* of what they were planning. They shut themselves in the living-room that evening, muttering in low voices. My brother Adam was in there with them and I could hear him talking, but I couldn't tell what he was saying. Because of his cerebral palsy, he uses a computerised voicebox to help him speak, and it was difficult to hear him through the door.

"You mean we can put our designs on your

computer, and work on them there?" I heard Kenny say. "Mega!"

They all charged over to the door then, and I had to run for it. They went to Adam's bedroom, and I hung around outside for a bit, trying to find out what was going on. Kenny came out and saw me, so then Adam put his stereo on really loudly and I couldn't hear a thing.

Next morning, my mum made me shut myself in the bathroom when everyone arrived, but I just caught a glimpse of them carrying lots of bags and boxes of stuff, before she shut the door. I hung around in the bathroom for about ten minutes, and when I came out, I found that they'd pinned a curtain over my bedroom door, so I couldn't see in.

"Go away, Rosie!" said Kenny, poking her head round it. "You know you're not allowed to see it until it's finished!"

"But it's killing me!" I protested.

"Tough!" Frankie looked round the curtain then too, and I noticed she had gold paint on her hands.

"Are you doing it in gold?" I asked eagerly, but they just stuck their tongues out at me, and disappeared.

It was *terrible*. I was dying to see how my bedroom was coming along, but I couldn't. Then I started to wonder what would happen if I didn't like it. I wouldn't be able to say so, because I'd hurt the others' feelings, so I'd be stuck with it. I was getting pretty worried by this time, so I went to the park with Adam in his wheelchair and Jenny, just to get out of the house.

That evening, after everyone had gone home, I *did* try to sneak a quick look. I was sharing Tiffany's room, but I crept along the landing when everyone else was asleep, just to see if I could get a peek. I pulled the curtain aside, but when I tried the door, it was locked. I was disgusted. Fancy locking the door! Didn't they trust me or something?

Everyone came back bright and early the next morning, and after a while, I could hear the sound of furniture being moved about, which drove me *crazy*. If they were putting the furniture back into place, they had to be close to finishing, I told myself hopefully. But it seemed ages until I heard footsteps on the stairs, and Fliss, Frankie, Kenny and Lyndz burst into the living-room, beaming all over their faces.

"We've finished!" they chorused.

"Really?" I jumped out of my seat, my heart beginning to pound. I just hoped I liked it! And if I didn't, I hoped I could fool everyone into *thinking* I did…

The others dragged me upstairs, where our mums and dads were waiting outside the room. Everyone was covered in gold and purple paint, so I guessed those were the colours they'd used. I was feeling pretty jittery by now, so I took a deep breath.

"Can I go in?"

Kenny and Fliss pulled the curtain aside for me, and I stepped into my new bedroom.

It felt like walking into a place I'd never been to before, because it just looked so totally different. The walls were papered in purple and gold, and everything had been painted to match, even my cupboards. There were big gold flower stencils on my wardrobe doors and above the picture rail, and billowy white curtains at the windows. My bed had been painted gold and purple too, and stencilled, and someone had fixed a white canopy to the ceiling which hung over the head of the bed. A matching purple and gold throw lay across the duvet. There was a purple paper lampshade, and a bunch of purple and gold flowers in a vase in the fireplace. I stared and stared. I just couldn't take it all in.

"Do you like it?" Kenny asked anxiously.

I found my voice at last. "I love it!" And I wasn't pretending either! It was the most gorgeous bedroom I'd ever seen in my whole life!

"Oh, good!" Fliss sounded relieved. "Do you like the stencils? They were my idea!"

"I painted the bed," Lyndz chimed in.

"With a little help from me!" said her dad with a grin.

"I painted the cupboards," Frankie added.

102

"And Kenny – well, Kenny just got in the way, as usual!"

"Zip it, Frankie!" Kenny gave her a shove. "I've got pretty good at wallpapering!"

"I think you've all done a brilliant job!" I said happily. "Now the next thing we've got to do is have our very first sleepover in it…"

We aren't usually allowed to have sleepovers on Sunday nights because of school the next day and all that, so we had to nag our parents a bit, but eventually they gave in. The others dashed home to clean up and get their sleepover stuff, and a few hours later we were all sitting round my new bedroom in our pyjamas, scoffing our midnight feast.

"I think I ought to buy some purple and gold pyjamas to match my room!" I said, nicking one of Kenny's crisps.

"Get you!" Kenny elbowed me in the ribs. "You'll be too posh for the Sleepover Club at this rate!"

"Yeah, maybe we should *all* design and decorate our bedrooms now!" Frankie suggested, munching a chocolate biscuit.

"I don't reckon our parents would be up for that," Fliss said. "My mum got home and went straight to bed! She said she was never doing any decorating ever again!"

"What shall we do now?" Lyndz asked as she snaffled the last few crisps. "Shall we play a game or something?"

"No, er – I want to say something first," I muttered. I stood up, and cleared my throat. "Um – I just wanted to say thank you for designing my bedroom, and I think you're the coolest friends in the whole world— aargh!"

I saw Kenny pick her pillow up, but I wasn't quick enough to dodge it. It hit me full in the face, and I screamed.

"You twit, Kenny! I'm going to get you for that!" I grabbed one of my pillows, and charged across the room.

"Brill – a pillow fight!" yelled Frankie, catching hold of the other pillow and swiping Fliss across the backside with it. Fliss scuttled across the room to get her own pillow, and got attacked by me and Kenny on the way. Meanwhile Frankie and Lyndz were doing their best to knock each other off my bed.

We were right in the middle of the action, when my mum put her head round the door, the cordless phone in her hand.

"Rosie? Your dad's just got back from Majorca, and he wants to talk to you."

I scrambled across the room and took the phone, managing to avoid a swipe round the head from Frankie's pillow. "Hello, Dad?" I gabbled breathlessly.

"Hello, Rosie," my dad said. He sounded a bit apologetic. "Listen, love, I'm sorry about letting you down last week. I was thinking of coming over tomorrow to make a start on your bedroom. What do you say?"

I began to laugh. I couldn't help it. "Yeah, come round tomorrow, Dad!" I said, and switched the phone off. He was in for a big surprise!

So that's the story of how I got my new bedroom! I bet you've been just as fed up as the others, listening to me moaning about it all the time, haven't you? Not any more though. My new bedroom's the business! Why don't you come round sometime and see for yourself?

Got to go now.

Catch you later!

The Sleepover Club
Surfs the Net

Frankie is hooked up to the Internet on her home computer and Rosie finds a competition to design a Home Page, with fab prizes for the winners and runners-up.

The Home Page has to be for a club that the entrants belong to. It takes clever Frankie to point out that they do all belong to a club — the Sleepover Club! After much cutting and sticking and staying up late, the girls' entry is ready for posting, but will it reach the competition organisers on time?

Pack up your sleepover kit and drop in on the fun!

0 00 675445-7

Sleepover Girls on Screen

Fliss perguades the rest of her friends to come with her when she goes to audition for a TV commercial. All starts well with a great sleepover, but trouble brews when all the Sleepover pals try for the same commercial. And Fliss isn't happy about it at all...

Pack up your sleepover kit and drop in on the fun!

000675446-5

Sleepover Girls and Friends

Mega news! The Spanish students that the Sleepover Club met on holiday are coming to stay. All sorts of fab activities are planned and the exchange gets off to a great start... until the two groups of friends fall out. What's gone wrong? And what have the M&Ms got to do with it?

Pack up your sleepover kit and have fun in the sun!

000675423-6

Anastasia Again!

The suburbs!" said Anastasia. "We're moving to the suburbs? I can't believe that you would actually do such a thing to me. I'm going to kill myself. As soon as I finish this chocolate pudding, I'm going to jump out of the window."

But Anastasia comes to grips with her misgivings much better than she could imagine, particularly when her fears that her goldfish might not like the suburbs prove to be unfounded.... And when she meets Steve, the tennis player from down the street, life in the suburbs begins to look like a pretty good thing afer all...

Anastasia Krupnik

Anastasia opened her green notebook and, in a secret corner, very small, she wrote the most terrible name she could think of. She closed the notebook, and smiled.

Anastasia Krupnik is ten, and two very important things are happening to her: A small pink wart appears on her left thumb: and she discovers that she'll soon be having a quite unnecessary baby brother.

Serious action is called for, but the only reason she hasn't left home yet is that she has been allowed to choose the baby's name...